MAHALIA JACKSON

Gospel Singer and Civil Rights Champion

Written by
Montrew Dunham

Illustrated by
Cathy Morrison

ISBN 9781882859382 (hardback)
ISBN 9781882859399 (paperback)

Patria Press, Inc.
PO Box 752
Carmel, IN 46082
Phone 888-859-8221
Website: www.patriapress.com

Printed and bound in the United States of America

Text originally published by the Bobbs-Merrill Company, 1974, in the Childhood of Famous Americans Series® The Childhood of Famous Americans Series® is a registered trademark of Simon & Schuster, Inc.

Publishers Cataloguing-in-Publication Data:

Dunham, Montrew.
Mahalia Jackson : gospel singer and civil rights champion / written by Montrew Dunham ; illustrated by Cathy Morrison. – 2nd ed. – Carmel, IN : Patria Press, 2003.
p. ; cm.
(Young patriots series ; 7)
Audience: ages 8-12.
"Text originally published by the Bobbs-Merrill Company, 1974, in the Childhood of Famous Americans Series." –T.p. verso.
Contents: Early days in New Orleans – A new home – A busy day for Mahalia – A trip to the levee – From church to sugar mill – A Christmas to remember – No business in show business – Joy and sadness – Big move to Chicago – Starting a singing career – Mahalia sings as a soloist – Only gospel singing – Singing my own way.
ISBN: 9781882959382
9781882859399 (pbk.)

1. Jackson, Mahalia, 1911-1972–Juvenile literature. 2. Jackson, Mahalia, 1911–1972–Childhood and youth–Juvenile literature. 3. Gospel musicians–United States–Biography–Juvenile literature. 4. [Jackson, Mahalia, 1911–1972. 5. Singers. 6. African Americans–Biography. 7. Women--Biography.] I. Morrison, Cathy. II. Title.

ML3930.J2 D86 2003 2003100641
782.25/4/092–dc21 0306

Edited by Harold Underdown
Design by TM Design

Contents

Illustrations

Dedication

To my father, Albert Howard Goetz

Chapter 1

Early Days in New Orleans

One Saturday Mahalia Jackson skipped down the dirt road after her ten-year-old brother. "Peter," she cried, "wait for me."

Peter was on his way to the levee along the Mississippi River. He looked back at his five-year-old sister, playing along after him. "Hurry up, Halie," he called.

Mahalia didn't really care whether she caught up with him or not. Mostly she enjoyed skipping along barefooted in the fine dirt. Gradually the dust formed a light brown coating on her feet which looked like a pair of shoes. She laughed and called to her brother, "Wait for me, Peter. Wait to see my new shoes."

By now Peter was running up the levee. He called back to Mahalia. "What crazy talk! You don't have new shoes."

Of course, Mahalia knew that she was only pretending. She laughed and looked at her shoes of dust again. She was very happy with those shoes.

She was happy too to be away from home. The Jackson family lived in a little three-room house in a district called the Front of the Town. Their neighbors included other African-Americans and immigrants from Europe. All of them were poor and had to work hard to make a living. Mahalia Jackson was born October 26, 1911, on Water Street. Her father, John Andrew Jackson, was pastor of the Mount Moriah Baptist Church. During the week, he worked part-time as a stevedore, helping to load and unload boats at docks along the river, and part-time as a barber.

Since Mahalia's family didn't have much money, she and Peter didn't just play at the levee. While they were there, they usually gathered driftwood to burn in the kitchen stove, or caught crabs, shrimp, and little alligators to take home for their mother to cook.

Today, after Mahalia quit admiring her make-believe shoes, she ran fast to catch up with Peter on the levee. Peter already had gone on down to the edge of the river. He was peering into the water, hoping to catch some little critter to take home for their mother to cook for supper that evening.

Mahalia sat down on the levee and looked at the muddy Mississippi. The water moved slowly but steadily along, its surface shining in the sunlight.

As Mahalia sat on the levee, she could see big boats tied up at the river docks a short distance away. She wondered whether her father was there, working with other men to load and unload the boats. She wondered what they were putting into the boats or taking out of them.

Mahalia closed her eyes and listened to the sounds of the city. She could hear the loud toots of boats traveling up and down the river and from farther away the shrill whistles of railroad locomotives. In between she could hear soft gentle music coming from nearby streets. The whole city seemed to be filled with colorful and exciting sounds.

Soon Mahalia jumped to her feet and ran on down to Peter at the edge of the water. He was intently watching a small alligator stretched out in the warm sunshine. He pointed to a stick, which Mahalia promptly picked up and handed to him. He raised the stick and brought it down with a sharp crack on the alligator's head.

Peter and Mahalia now started home, with Peter carrying the little alligator. When they reached the house, Mama asked, "What are you bringing home from the river?"

"A little alligator for supper," Peter replied proudly.

That evening the Jackson family had a tasty feast of alligator tail, baked and smothered with onions and herbs. Soon after supper, Peter and Mahalia got ready for bed. The next day was Sunday, and they would have to get up early to go to church. Their father would preach there, as he did every Sunday morning.

When Mahalia climbed into bed, she went right to sleep. A couple of hours later, however, sounds and movements around her woke her up. She could hear raindrops pattering on the roof. Her mother was bringing buckets and pans to catch dribbles of water leaking through.

Mahalia peeked out to the soft light coming in from the kitchen and caught a glimpse of her father sitting by the table. She watched him as he read his big bible and made notes on a sheet of paper beside him. Proudly she realized that he was preparing his sermon to deliver at church services the next morning. Somehow just watching him and being close to him made her feel safer when everything was dark and stormy outside.

Suddenly a big cold drop of water splattered on her face, followed by another and another. She sat up and shouted, "Mama! Mama! I'm getting wet from the rain!"

Her mother came running in with a small washpan to catch the water. "Get up," she said calmly. "We'll have to move your bed to the other side of the room."

Mahalia hopped out to help her mother push the bed away from the leak in the roof. Then she climbed back in, hoping no more drops would fall on her. "Now go back to sleep and forget the rain," said her mother.

At first Mahalia was too excited to go to sleep again. For a while she lay listening to the steady patter of raindrops falling on the roof and the frequent splatter of water dripping into the buckets and pans. Finally the sounds lulled her to sleep.

When she woke up the next morning, the sun was shining and the rain was over. "It's time to get up, Halie," called her mother. "Hurry to get dressed so I can fix your hair before we go to church."

Mahalia dressed quickly and ran to her mother, who started to brush and braid her hair. At first she stood quietly, but soon she began to jerk and flinch. "Quit wriggling," scolded her mother, giving her a little tap on the side of her head.

"I can't help it, Mama," replied Mahalia. "You're making my braids too tight."

Just then Peter pushed open the ragged screen door and called, "I'm going on, Mama."

"No, wait," replied his mother. "Mahalia and I are ready to go, too."

When they reached the church, Papa was already standing up front by the pulpit. As usual, Mama sat

The members of the congregation always stood while they sang. Mahalia stood along with the others, only she stood on the seat where she could see.

in a pew near the front, with Peter and Mahalia in the pew in front of her.

Soon the church was completely filled. The room was steaming hot, and flies droned in and out of the open windows. Mahalia watched her father proudly as he preached his sermon. Beads of sweat rolled down his face as he spoke and waved his arms. Everybody sat quietly and nobody seemed to mind the heat or the flies.

A choir director led the singing during the services, and one of the ladies played the church organ. The members of the congregation always stood while they sang. Mahalia stood along with the others, only she stood on the seat where she could see.

She loved to sing and knew most of the songs well from singing them over and over again. As she sang this Sunday morning, one grown-up person after another stopped singing just to listen to her. Finally she was the only person left singing in the entire church.

At the end of the services, the choir director said to Mahalia's father, "May we have Mahalia sing in the choir?" In reply, her father smiled and said, "I reckon so, if you want her, but she is a mighty little girl to sing in a choir."

Chapter 2

A New Home

One morning when Mahalia awoke, hot sunlight was already pouring through her window. She pulled on her dress and quickly ran to the kitchen. "Mama! Mama!" she called on the way. "I'm hungry!"

"Mama didn't get up this morning," said Peter seriously. "She's sick in bed."

Mahalia stopped short and looked at her brother. He was sitting at the kitchen table, eating corn bread and molasses.

"What do you mean, Mama's sick in bed?" she asked. She could hardly believe her brother's words.

"Just what I said," answered Peter. "She was too sick to get up this morning."

Mahalia found the kitchen strange and empty without her mother. "Mama, where are you?" she called, running into her mother's room.

"I'm right here, Halie," answered her mother in a tired voice. "Don't worry, I'll soon be all right again."

She lifted her head a little from the pillow and tried to smile. "Go on and get your breakfast," she said. "Peter will help you find something to eat."

Mahalia went back to the kitchen, feeling sad and worried. This was the first time she had ever had to get her own breakfast. She was no longer hungry but finally took a piece of crumbly corn bread.

"Put the bread on a plate," scolded Peter. "You're dropping crumbs all over the floor."

Mahalia meekly put the corn bread on a plate and placed it on the table. She got out a pitcher of milk and put an empty glass beside her plate. Then she started to pour milk from the pitcher into the glass, but somehow she let the pitcher drop to the floor. Fortunately it didn't break, but it splashed milk in all directions.

Mahalia bit her lips to keep from crying. She reached down and grabbed the pitcher, trying to rescue some of the milk. "What's going on out there?" called her mother.

"Halie dropped the milk pitcher and spilled milk all over the floor," answered Peter.

"But I didn't break the pitcher, and I'll wipe up all the milk."

"Wipe up what you can," said Mama, "and I'll clean up the rest when I feel better."

Day after day the children hoped their mother would get better, but she grew steadily worse.

By now Mama, propped up in bed, was listening closely to Uncle Porter's story.

Papa had to go to work every day and Peter went to school. Mama's sisters came to visit and to help out. Mahalia helped these aunts all she could.

Mama's oldest brother, Uncle Porter, also came to help. He knew more about the family than anybody else, and had helped Mama and her sisters come to New Orleans to live. Mahalia asked him many questions.

Uncle Porter, Mama, and all their brothers and sisters had been born on a former slave plantation. Their father had been a sharecropper on the plantation. He had grown rice on the owner's land and received a share of the harvest for his work. All his children had worked with him to help raise the rice.

Once when Uncle Porter was visiting Mama, Mahalia asked, "Uncle Porter, how did you ever get to New Orleans?"

"That's a long story," replied Uncle Porter, taking her on his knee. "One time when I was growing up, I got mad at the plantation owner and he got mad at me. I talked mean to him and he talked mean to me."

"Did you have a fight?" asked Mahalia.

"No, but right then and there I made up my mind to leave the plantation," said Uncle Porter. "I got a job on a riverboat and learned to be a cook. Then for years I cooked on riverboats that traveled south to New Orleans."

"Now tell me about bringing Mama here to New Orleans," begged Mahalia.

"Well, after I got acquainted here, I went back to the plantation to get some of my sisters," replied Uncle Porter.

By now Mama, propped up in bed, was listening closely to Uncle Porter's story. Suddenly, he turned to her and asked, "Charity, do you remember how I brought you here?"

"I surely do," replied Mama. "You brought me here on a steamboat. Then you got me a job as a maid at Captain Rucker's house."

"The captain was a good friend of mine," said Uncle Porter. "I made my first trip down the Mississippi River on his steamboat."

"Yes, he really liked you," said Mama. "He used to call you his colored son."

Uncle Porter laughed. "That's right," he said. "He was white, but he took me into his house and finished raising me just like his own children."

Mahalia sat down on a little stool and listened to her mother and uncle talk about the cotton plantation and their first years in New Orleans. She tried to keep quiet because Mama seemed to enjoy talking.

As the days went on, Mama grew weaker and weaker. Everybody wanted to help her, but nobody was able to do anything to make her better. Finally one day she died.

All the relatives gathered and took Mama's body by train and boat back to the country neighborhood where she had grown up. They had services for her in the little church which she had attended as a child. Then they buried her in the little cemetery by the church.

At the cemetery, Mahalia looked curiously at her father's dark face, wet with tears. She was too young to fully understand why he and all the others were crying. Somehow she felt that when she returned home, her mother would be there just as she had always been before.

The relatives gathered at the railroad station to return to New Orleans. They talked seriously and softly and stepped over to tell Papa how sorry they felt because Mama had died. Some asked him what he planned to do about Mahalia and Peter. Mahalia felt so lonely that she climbed up on the bench in the station just to be closer to her father.

Soon the train came, and Mahalia's father picked her up and carried her into a coach. Peter and all the relatives followed and sat in seats close by. Before long the relatives began once more to talk among themselves. Mahalia listened closely because she could tell they were talking about her and Peter.

One aunt said, "I would be glad to take them to raise, but I don't have enough room."

Another aunt said, "One of us could take Peter and another one can take Mahalia. I'll be glad to take Peter, if one of you will take Mahalia."

A third aunt said, "Well, if you will take Peter, I'll be glad to take Mahalia."

Finally a fourth aunt, whom everybody called Aunt Duke, spoke up. She was older than the others and spoke with authority. "Peter and Mahalia should stay together as brother and sister," she said. "I'll take both of them."

Aunt Duke's statement settled everything. All the others, including Papa, agreed that this would be best for the children. Aunt Duke was a dark brown-skinned woman with a firm, determined look in her eyes. Often Mahalia felt as if she were looking straight through her.

Within a few days Peter and Mahalia moved in with Aunt Duke and Uncle Emanuel, wondering what their new life would be like. Both knew, however, that they had no other choice.

Chapter 3

A Busy Day for Mahalia

"Halie! Halie!" called Aunt Duke one summer morning. "Get out of bed and come to breakfast. Nobody in this house can lie around in bed in the morning. Do your work early while it's still cool."

Mahalia sat up in bed, stretched, and sighed. Living here certainly was different from living back home with Mama. Aunt Duke wouldn't let anyone stay in bed past sunrise.

When Mahalia reached the kitchen, she took her place at the table with Peter and Uncle Emanuel. Aunt Duke, dressed in the blue uniform she wore at work, stood waiting by the stove. Quickly she placed two fried eggs and a piece of fresh hot cornbread on Mahalia's plate. Uncle Emanuel handed Mahalia a pitcher of brown molasses to pour on her cornbread. Peter was busy eating, because he was working as a yard boy during the summer.

Before Aunt Duke left for work, she gave Mahalia

strict instructions on what to do during the day. "First, wash and wipe the kitchen dishes and put them away," she said. "Then scrub the kitchen floor. Be sure to clean all the corners. Afterwards go down the street and get a big bag of Spanish moss, so we can stuff a bed mattress when I get home."

After Aunt Duke left, Mahalia, Peter, and Uncle Emanuel continued to sit and talk. Peter told them about the work he would have to do as a yard boy during the day. "It won't be long before school will start again," he said. "Then I won't have a chance to work during the day to earn money."

"Yes, this fall I'll be old enough to start school," chimed in Mahalia. "I can hardly wait to learn to read."

"You're smart and I'm sure you will learn real fast," said Peter, as he left.

Uncle Emanuel remained at the table with Mahalia. "I still have time to work in the garden a while before I need to leave," he said. "How would you like to come out to help me after you finish doing the dishes?"

"Oh, good!" cried Mahalia. "That will be fun.

Carefully she scraped the sticky molasses from the plates and stacked them on the table. She placed a big tin dishpan in the sink for washing the dishes and a smaller pan for rinsing them. She poured hot water from the kettle on the stove into the dishpan and the rinsing pan. Then she reached up to the handle of the pump at the end of the sink and pumped cold water into the dishpan.

She took down a bar of homemade soap and swished it about in the water to make it sudsy. She washed the dirty dishes in the soapy water and rinsed them in the pan of hot clear water. Then she wiped each one dry with a clean cloth.

After she had put away all the dishes, she emptied both pans of water out the back door. Then she ran from the house to the garden and called, "Here I am, Uncle Emanuel, ready to help."

"Good," cried Uncle Emanuel. "You may pull weeds along the row of beans over there at the side of the garden."

Mahalia ran to one end of the row and started to work. She had learned that she should grab a weed next to the ground and try to pull it out by the roots.

As she worked, the sun rose higher, and the rays from the sun became hotter and hotter. Mahalia began to suffer from the heat, but she kept right on pulling weeds. She looked over and could see sweat rolling down Uncle Emanuel's face, but he kept working.

Mahalia eagerly looked toward the end of the row. At last she pulled the last weed and threw it to the ground. "There, Uncle Emanuel," she called. "I have finished my row."

Uncle Emanuel looked at the row she had weeded. "You surely have done a fine job, Halie," he said, "just as good as I could have done. Now go on into the house out of the hot sun."

Uncle Emanuel rubbed his face and neck with a big red handkerchief. He stood for a moment to admire the neat healthy rows of corn, tomatoes, beans, okra, mustard greens, and cabbage growing in his garden. "This is a good place to live," he said. "From this garden we get all the vegetables that we need. From the river we get all the fish, crabs, and shrimp that we need."

"And we have Aunt Duke to bake good cakes and pies," added Mahalia.

Uncle Emanuel laughed and agreed. "Yes, Aunt Duke is a mighty fine cook," he said. "You're a good weed puller, and someday I predict you'll be a mighty fine cook, too."

Mahalia felt happy as she watched Uncle Emanuel walk down the street. Before long he turned and waved at her, and she waved back at him.

As she walked back toward the house she noticed her old rag doll resting on the step. "Oh, Debra Sue!" she cried, reaching over to pick her up.

This doll was homemade, with black buttons for eyes. Her hair was grass held in place by a sock pulled over her head for a cap. When Mahalia picked up the doll, she noticed that her hair was brown and withered. "Your hair is dried out," she said. "I'll have to get you some new hair."

She plucked tall blades of green grass and neatly braided it. She held her mouth tightly and grimly as she worked.

When she finished the braid, she removed the sock and old braid from the doll's head. Carefully she replaced it with the new braid and pulled on the sock to keep it in place. Finally she held up the doll to admire her new hair and started to rock her gently back and forth.

Suddenly she remembered that Aunt Duke wanted her to scrub the kitchen floor. She jumped up and leaned the doll against the back step. "Now, Debra Sue, take a nap while I do my work," she said. "I'll be back in a little while."

She ran into the house, poured some lye in a bucket of water, and got out a big scrub brush. Moments later she dropped to her knees and started to scrub. Her hands smarted from the lye in the water, but she kept right on scrubbing.

She remembered that Aunt Duke had told her to scrub all the dark corners, so she did them first, and then she moved to the center of the floor. As she scrubbed, she kept backing up on her knees. Finally, when her feet touched the screen door, she knew that she was almost done.

Quickly she jumped to her feet, emptied the water out the back door, and put away the bucket and brush. As she started out the back door to play with Debra Sue, Aunt Duke called to her from the front door, "Halie, have you brought home the moss? I have come home early to fill the mattress."

At this question, Mahalia's heart almost leaped into her mouth. "No, but I'll go after it right now," she replied meekly.

Aunt Duke's face had an angry look. She went to a closet and pulled out a big basket. "Here, take this basket and bring it back completely full," she said in a stern tone.

Mahalia rushed down the street, carrying the big basket. She enjoyed pulling moss from the branches of gnarled old trees. As she ran, she heard someone calling to her from one of the houses, "Halie, where are you going?"

She saw an Italian neighbor boy, Gino, sitting on his front step. "I'm going to get moss," she answered.

"May I go, too?" asked Gino.

"Sure," replied Mahalia. "You can help me."

Soon Mahalia and Gino came to a long row of oak trees with long bunches of Spanish moss hanging from their branches. Mahalia looked up and hardly knew where to begin picking. She pulled down several bunches and stuffed them into the basket.

Gino, close beside her, also started to pull down bunches of moss. Once he pulled extra hard on a bunch and when it came loose, he fell backward on the ground, covered with moss. Mahalia looked down at him and laughed.

Before long Mahalia swung herself up to the first branch of a tree and started to pull down more moss and drop it to the ground. She climbed higher and higher in the tree. Down below Gino picked up the moss and put it into the basket.

Finally Mahalia stood on a branch and paused to rest against the trunk of the tree. The beauty of the sunlit branches, draped with shimmering, gray-green moss, fascinated her. A gentle breeze fanned her face, and she felt joyful and happy. "Come on down," called Gino down below. "What are you doing?"

"I'm just resting and enjoying myself," replied Mahalia. "Everything is so beautiful up here I don't want to come down."

"Well, come on," he replied. "We have all the moss we can carry."

Mahalia and Gino started home with the heavy basket, each holding a handle.

Gino helped carry the heavy basket of moss to the back door of the house. Mahalia pulled open the door and dragged the basket on into the house. "Here's your basket of moss, Aunt Duke," she called.

Aunt Duke was waiting with all the materials they would need to make and stuff a mattress. She had several old cotton cement sacks to sew together to make a mattress cover. She had a bag of cornhusks, which they would use along with the Spanish moss to stuff the mattress.

Mahalia stood quietly while Aunt Duke pushed a twine cord through the eye of a long needle and tied a knot at the end of the cord. She handed the threaded needle to Mahalia and threaded another needle for herself. Then the two of them started to stitch together the old cotton sacks to make a mattress cover.

Aunt Duke pushed her needle in and out of the cloth quickly and easily. Mahalia could only push hers in and out of the cloth slowly and awkwardly. She wondered how Aunt Duke could sew so swiftly, but finally she managed to finish a seam. Aunt Duke carefully inspected it and half-smiled in approval.

They were ready to fill the new mattress. Aunt Duke held one end open while Mahalia dumped in first an armful of corn husks and then an armful of moss. "Push them into the mattress as far as you can reach," said Aunt Duke. "We must stuff it as full as possible."

Mahalia shoved the cornhusks and moss in as far as she could reach with her short arms. Before long

They were ready to fill the new mattress. Aunt Duke held one end open while Mahalia dumped in first an armful of corn husks and then an armful of moss.

Aunt Duke held up the mattress and shook the cornhusks and moss toward the bottom. Then Mahalia stuffed in more of the cornhusks and moss, and Aunt Duke stuffed in still more. At last Aunt Duke sewed up the open end of the mattress and the job was done.

Mahalia looked curiously at the new plump mattress. "Climb on it and see how soft it feels," said Aunt Duke.

Joyfully Mahalia jumped on the mattress and started to bounce up and down. She felt so happy that she giggled with every bounce.

Chapter 4

A Trip to the Levee

In the fall after Mahalia went to live with Aunt Duke, she started school. Each weekday she walked to and from school with Peter and a few neighborhood children. She thought that going to school was important because now she could learn to read.

Her closest friend at school was a girl named Sally Lou. One afternoon, after school, Sally Lou asked Mahalia to go to the levee with her. "May I go to the levee with Sally Lou?" Mahalia called to Aunt Duke.

"Yes, but don't stay very long," answered Aunt Duke. "I'll expect you back home by the time the sun sets."

The two girls ran on, but Aunt Duke called extra orders to Mahalia. "Take a bag with you to fill with pieces of driftwood," she said. "I need wood for the stove."

Mahalia ran back and Aunt Duke handed her a big burlap bag for carrying the wood. Sally Lou ran home to get a bag so she could bring home some crabs or shrimp for her mother to cook. Then both girls skipped on toward the levee.

When they reached the levee, they climbed to the top to look up and down the river. They watched steamboats with paddle wheels stirring up the water and leaving dripping spray behind them. They saw other steamboats tied up at nearby docks, where stevedores were busy loading and unloading them.

Sally Lou soon pulled a small bucket from her bag and started to scoop up crabs from the edge of the water. She scooped them up and dumped them into the burlap bag.

Mahalia began to look for pieces of driftwood. She noticed several pieces floating out in the water. She picked up a pole and tried to pull them toward her.

The pole was too short to reach the pieces of wood, so she stepped out into the water. Her feet sank deep in the soft, oozy mud, but she managed to reach the driftwood. Then she used the pole to help push herself back out of the mud.

She carried the wet pieces of wood to the top of the levee and spread them out to dry. Finally she wiped her muddy hands and feet in the nearby grass and sat down to rest.

Gradually her thoughts turned to herself. She wondered whether she always would live in New Orleans,

Sally Lou soon pulled a small bucket from her bag and started to scoop up crabs from the edge of the water.

or whether she would live someplace else. She hoped that she wouldn't have to grow up to just do housework all her life, as many African-American women had to do in New Orleans at that time. Now that she was going to school, maybe she could learn to do other things, too.

The great orange sun slipped down slowly in the west until it left only a golden streak across the river.

Mahalia arose and started to put the pieces of firewood into her burlap bag. Sally Lou joined her, and the two girls took off with their two loaded bags.

When they were almost home, they heard jazz music coming from a dance hall down the street. Even though Mahalia was dragging a bag of heavy firewood, she started to keep time to the rhythm of the music. She often had wished that she could go down the street to peek into the dance hall, but she knew that Aunt Duke wouldn't let her.

Aunt Duke was standing in the door waiting for the girls to return home. When she saw Mahalia swinging along in time to the jazz music, she was extremely angry. "Halie!" she shouted. "Get on inside the house where you belong."

Dutifully Mahalia walked into the house, dragging the bag of heavy firewood. She still could hear the lively music and could scarcely keep from dancing. "Is that wood dry?" asked Aunt Duke.

Mahalia reached her hand into the bag and felt the wood. "No, it isn't, Aunt Duke," she replied. "I spread it out on the levee for a while to dry in the sun, but it is still wet."

"Then put it outside by the back step to dry," ordered Aunt Duke.

Slowly Mahalia carried the wood outside and leaned it against the house. Once more she paused to listen to the swinging jazz music coming from the dance hall. Aunt Duke looked out, shook her head, and sighed. "All right," she said, "You may sit here on the step and listen, but don't you dare leave."

Mahalia sat down on the top step while the darkness of night gathered around her. She didn't notice the darkness because she was charmed by the music. She just sat and listened, contented and happy.

Before long, she began to hear music coming from the church next door. She listened closely as the members of the congregation sang. Besides the singing, she could hear drums, cymbals, and tambourines gloriously beating out the rhythm. Soon this beautiful music completely drowned out the jazz music coming from the dance hall.

Through the open windows of the church, Mahalia could see the shadows of the members of the congregation as they started to clap their hands and stamp their feet while they sang. Soon she rose to her feet and began to sing, clap her hands, and stomp her feet along with them. Aunt Duke came to the door and smiled.

Chapter 5

From Church to Sugar Mill

One Friday morning in summer while Mahalia was on vacation from school, she ran happily to Mount Moriah. She and other children cleaned the church to get it ready for the weekend services. In return for their help, they were allowed to take turns ringing the bell on Sunday.

When Mahalia entered the church, one of the churchwomen handed her a big dust rag. "Good morning, Halie," she said. "I have an important job for you today. You may take this rag and dust the furniture."

When she finished dusting the pews, she went up front to dust the altar. She moved timidly because she knew that this was a place to kneel and pray.

After Mahalia finished dusting the altar, she stepped up to the pulpit. To her this pulpit was important because her own father stood here each Sunday to preach.

Finally she left the pulpit and moved over to the organ, which also was important to her, because she loved the music it made. First she wiped off the stool in front of the organ, and then dusted the front of the organ and the keys.

All the while she sat dusting, she wished that she could run her fingers over the keys to make them play music. Even though she didn't know how to play the organ, nothing could keep her from singing. Suddenly she whirled herself around on the organ stool and started to sing one of her favorite songs. The churchwoman stood by and laughed. "I declare," she exclaimed, "you surely do love to sing."

She came over to inspect Halie's dusting. She wiped her fingers over different pieces of furniture but couldn't find any dust. "All right, Halie, you've done a fine job of dusting. For being so careful you may ring the church bell Sunday morning."

"Oh, thank you!" cried Mahalia. She was so happy that she ran home to tell Aunt Duke.

At home Aunt Duke was in no mood to listen to Mahalia. Instead she handed her a basket and said, "Here, take this basket and go over to the railroad tracks to pick up some lumps of coal for the kitchen stove."

Mahalia took the basket and started down the road toward the railroad tracks. A few houses away, she found her friend Sally Lou, swinging on the gate in front of her house. "Hello there, Halie," called Sally Lou. "Where are you going with that basket?"

"I'm going to the railroad tracks to pick up some chunks of coal for Aunt Duke," replied Mahalia. "Do you want to go along?"

Sally Lou ran inside to tell her mother and then back out to go along with Mahalia.

The two girls skipped along together. When they reached the railroad tracks, they started to pick up small lumps of coal, which had fallen from train cars. Before long Sally Lou called, "Stand back from the tracks, Halie. A train is coming toward us."

Mahalia looked up and saw a switch engine coming a short distance away. She dragged the basket off to one side on the grass.

The girls stood back from the tracks to watch the train go by. Soon the engine passed, belching out grey-blue smoke that trailed back over the cars it pulled. Now the girls eagerly waited for the caboose of the train to come by. They knew that friendly trainmen sometimes invited children to take rides to nearby factories. There the children could pick up juicy sticks of sugar cane to suck and chew.

Soon the caboose came, and the girls could see other children riding inside. A friendly trainman called and invited them to jump on. They ran quickly to the caboose and he helped them up the steps.

When the train reached the sugar factory, the two girls ran to a big stack of sugar cane. They looked about the stack to find stalks still filled with sweet juice. Finally they sat down at the edge of the stack to suck on a couple of sugar cane stalks.

Before long, the train was ready to start back up the track. “All aboard,” called the friendly trainman, and all the children climbed onto the caboose, carrying stalks of cane in their arms.

When the time came to get off, they jumped from the slow-moving caboose. The two girls then headed for home, munching the sweet pulp from the sugar cane stalks. Suddenly Gino and his friend Joe appeared and tried to take the stalks away from them.

Both girls started to fight. Mahalia flung her fists at Gino and grabbed him around the neck. She held him so tightly that he could scarcely breathe. “Please let me go,” he begged. “You’re choking me.”

“All right,” she said, “but don’t ever try anything like this again!” She pushed him and sent him rolling back on the ground.

Just then Joe, who had been fighting close by with Sally Lou, came over and threatened to hit her. She grabbed a stick of wood from the ground and shouted,

"Now run as fast as you can before I give you a good beating!"

Joe took one look at Mahalia's angry face and started to run down the street. Mahalia rushed over to Sally Lou, who was sitting exhausted under a tree. "Are you all right?" she asked.

"I guess so," replied Sally Lou, "but I'm certainly mad at those boys."

"So am I," said Mahalia. "If they want some sugar cane stalks, they should get their own."

Just as the girls were ready to start on, Sally Lou noticed a big torn place in Mahalia's dress. "Oh, my," she exclaimed, "you have a tear in your dress."

Mahalia looked down and saw the big tear near the bottom hem of her dress. "Now I'll really catch it when I reach home," she said.

As they started on again, Mahalia said, "I think I'll stop at the barbershop to see Papa."

Mahalia loved her father and tried to see him as often as possible. She saw him on Sunday morning when he preached and during the week whenever she could at the barbershop. He worked there late each afternoon and evening.

When they reached the barbershop, Sally Lou ran on home and Mahalia stepped inside. "Hello there, Chocolate Drop," called her father. "What happened to you?" he asked when he saw the torn dress.

"Sally Lou and I just had a fight with Gino and Joe," she explained. "They tried to take our sugar cane away from us. Usually they're good friends, but now we're mad at them."

Papa smiled and went on cutting hair. Mahalia sat down in a nearby chair and told him all about her train ride to and from the sugar cane factory. Finally she jumped up and said, "I guess I'd better go on home now. Aunt Duke will be looking for me."

Her father stopped cutting hair and came over to kiss her good-by. He handed her a carefully folded one-dollar bill and told her to give it to Aunt Duke. He tried to give Aunt Duke as much money as he could to pay her for keeping Mahalia and Peter.

The moment Mahalia walked into the house, Aunt Duke noticed the tear in her dress. "How did that happen?" she demanded angrily. Then without hesitating, she went right on to ask, "And where is the basket of coal?"

Mahalia was stunned. In all the excitement she had completely forgotten about the basket of coal. "It's down by the railroad track, Aunt Duke," she replied. "I'll go back to get it and bring it as quickly as I can."

She ran from the house and kept on running until she came to the place where she had boarded the caboose. All the way she kept wondering what she would do if someone had stolen the basket of

Papa smiled and went on cutting hair. Mahalia sat down in a nearby chair and told him all about her train ride to and from the sugar cane factory.

coal. Fortunately, when she arrived she found it right where she had left it.

On the way home, she held the basket in front of her, and got black coal dust all over her torn dress. She took the basket to the back door and called, "Here is your basket of coal, Aunt Duke."

Aunt Duke looked at Mahalia's torn and dirty dress and muttered, "Humph!" but asked no further questions. Instead she pointed to the kitchen table and said, "Sit down and eat your supper. Then take your bath and go to bed, so you'll be ready to go to church early tomorrow."

Friday evening always was a busy time at Aunt Duke's house. All the cooking had to be done for the weekend, because everybody spent both Saturday and Sunday attending services at the church. Everyone took baths and laid out their clean clothes. Then on Saturday morning they had to get up early for church.

Mahalia liked going to church for the weekend services. She hummed a tune as she took her bath and grinned as she watched Aunt Duke get out a clean dress for her to wear the next day. Finally she went to sleep, thinking of the fun she would have ringing the church bell on Sunday before Papa started to preach.

Chapter 6

A Christmas to Remember

Everybody in New Orleans was getting ready for Christmas. The school that Peter and Mahalia attended had closed for the holidays. Christmas trees and candles filled many windows, and people along the streets sang Christmas songs.

At night, Mahalia was too excited to sleep. Through the open door, she could see Aunt Duke busy in the kitchen, cooking different goodies for Christmas dinner. Every few minutes she bent down to open and close the oven door, and the odors of luscious foods drifted through the house.

Aunt Duke had been cooking for several days to get everything ready. Ordinarily she wanted Mahalia to help her with the cooking, but at Christmas time she shooed everybody out of the kitchen. At this time of the year she wanted to do everything by herself.

Before long Mahalia closed her eyes and listened to the people singing Christmas songs in the church next door. She wished she could climb out of bed and run over to join them. Finally when they started to sing a familiar song, she sang along with them.

The next day, the day before Christmas, was entirely different for Mahalia. Aunt Duke, who now was trying to wind up her cooking, called on Mahalia to bring many things that she needed. She still wanted her to stay completely out of the kitchen.

Once she called, "Mahalia, bring me that pan of eggs from the back porch."

Quickly Mahalia brought the pan of eggs and set it on the table. Then slyly she tiptoed over behind Aunt Duke to peek at a steamy pot of rich, creamy shrimp gumbo cooking on the stove. Aunt Duke noticed her and cried sternly, "Halie, get yourself out of the kitchen. Leave before I throw you out."

Aunt Duke kept on barking orders, but insisted on Mahalia staying outside. "Get me some water. Fetch some wood. Bring me some more eggs," she called in rapid succession.

Between errands, Mahalia stood at the kitchen door watching Aunt Duke work. At last she interrupted her to ask, "When will Uncle Porter get here for Christmas?"

"His train should come sometime late this afternoon," answered Aunt Duke. "He should arrive in time to go to church tonight."

Christmas trees and candles filled many windows, and people along the streets sang Christmas songs.

Mahalia was eager to see Uncle Porter again. She remembered how she had enjoyed seeing him when he had come to see Mama several years before. Now he was a cook in a diner on a railroad train and she hardly ever got to see him. He had to work nearly all the time.

Aunt Duke's son, Cousin Fred, was supposed to come for Christmas, too, but nobody knew when to expect him. He was a big, handsome young man who worked outside the city.

On Christmas Eve there were special services at the church. A big Christmas tree stood up front beside the pulpit. It was covered with small candles that flickered in the dimly lit room. Larger candles burned in the windows on both sides of the church. Mahalia's father preached a powerful sermon.

The organist pumped out joyful Christmas music. The whole church rang with singing, clapping of hands, and tapping of feet, and everybody was filled with the spirit of Christmas.

When the Christmas Eve services ended, Mahalia hesitated to leave. Sadly she watched the people put the candles out one by one. At last, when the church was completely dark, she started to cry. Somehow she felt as if a glorious experience had slipped away from her, never to be enjoyed again.

All the while Aunt Duke had watched Mahalia. Finally she walked over to her, threw her arms around her, and said, "Come, Halie. We can't stay here any longer. It's time to go home."

Mahalia was touched that Aunt Duke had waited for her. Together they walked slowly out of the darkened church toward home. Now and then Mahalia looked back as if hoping to find the church still filled with joyful words and music.

The following morning, which was Christmas, everybody went to church to celebrate again. Once more Mahalia's father preached, and once more she sang happily with the members of the congregation. Much of the time her voice rang out loudly and clearly above the voices of all the others. She clapped her hands and stamped her feet gaily as she joined in the singing.

After church all the relatives went back to Aunt Duke's for Christmas dinner. In the center of the table there was a roasted raccoon, stuffed with mushy sweet potatoes. Nearby there were platters of roast pork and roast goose. Scattered about there were bowls of shrimp gumbo and tasty vegetables. Out in the kitchen there were several kinds of rich pies and cakes, ready to be served.

At first all the uncles, aunts, and cousins were too busy eating to do much talking. Finally they began to talk and laugh. Everybody was happy to be together again.

From time to time Mahalia looked over admiringly at Cousin Fred, who wanted to try all the special foods his mother had prepared. He wore handsome clothes and looked more up-to-date than anybody at the table. Every little while he stopped eating to tell something funny that he had seen, heard, or done.

Uncle Porter told them about being a cook on a dining car. He explained that sometimes he cooked meals for four hundred persons a day riding on the train. "How could you possibly cook for that many people in such a small kitchen?" asked one of his sisters, shaking her head in doubt.

Uncle Porter threw back his head and laughed. "I wish you could see the fine meals that I prepare in my kitchen, " he said. "I know right where everything is and I can cook faster than any of you can cook in your homes."

Mahalia sat and listened, enjoying the time with her family at home.

Chapter 7

No Business in Show Business

All the winter evenings at Aunt Duke's home were about the same. Peter and Mahalia sat at the kitchen table to study their lessons. Uncle Emanuel usually sat in a rocking chair, resting or sleeping, and Aunt Duke sat in another rocking chair, sewing or mending clothes. One evening, they heard someone push open the door and call, "Hey, are you at home?"

Mahalia looked up and saw her father and two strangers standing in the doorway. She jumped up from the table, rushed over to him, and cried, "Oh, Papa! What a surprise!"

Her father stepped forward and held out his arms to embrace her. "Hello, Chocolate Drop," he cried, hugging her tightly.

Then he introduced the two strangers as his cousin Jeanette Burnette and her husband, Josie. Aunt Duke promptly invited them to go into the living room to sit down and talk.

Mahalia looked curiously at the fine clothes which Jeannette and Josie were wearing. Jeannette wore a gaudy red dress with matching gloves on her hands and slippers on her feet. Josie wore a striped suit with a white stiff-front shirt and shiny red silk tie. He had a red handkerchief tucked in his front coat pocket and carried a stiff derby hat.

"Who in the world are these people, wearing such fancy clothes?" Mahalia wondered. Papa had introduced Jeannette as his cousin and Josie as her husband, but she had never heard of them before.

After everybody was seated in the front room, Aunt Duke said, "Well, this is a surprise. What brings you to New Orleans?"

"We're traveling with Ma Rainey and will be here for a few days," replied Jeanette.

"Who is Ma Rainey?" asked Aunt Duke.

"She is a famous colored singer," replied Mahalia's father. "People often call her the 'Mama of the Blues.'"

"Yes, she travels about and puts on a show in a tent," explained Jeanette. "We travel with her and perform our act in her show."

Aunt Duke didn't offer any comment, but Mahalia, who sat next to her, heard her say, "Humph!" under her breath. She had told Mahalia many times she was very suspicious of show people. She thought they were too frivolous to do any good in the world.

Before long the conversation changed, and nothing more was said about the show. Mahalia knew some of the people they mentioned, but not many.

On Sunday morning Jeannette and Josie attended church services. When they entered the church, they sat directly in front of Mahalia and Aunt Duke. Everybody stared at them and wondered who they were.

They were decked out in clothes even finer than those they had worn when Mahalia first met them. Odors of rich perfume came from their clothes and spread about the room.

After her father started to preach, Mahalia kept twisting and turning to see more of Jeannette and Josie's fine clothes. Suddenly Aunt Duke gave her a hard poke in the side, leaned over, and whispered angrily, "Stop gawking at Jeannette and Josie. Sit quietly the way you're supposed to sit in church and listen to your father's preaching."

Mahalia nodded and tried to sit quietly in her seat. She looked at her father and pretended to listen, but actually she kept on thinking about Jeanette and Josie. She wondered what kind of act they had in Ma Rainey's show. What did they do in their act? Did they sing? Did they dance? Did they play musical instruments?

Mahalia's father concluded his sermon. The members of the congregation rose to their feet and started to sing "Amazing Grace, How Sweet It Sounds." They soon began to clap their hands and stamp their feet to the rhythm.

Mahalia sang with all the joy and ardor in her soul. Her voice rang out loudly and clearly above all the other voices in the room.

Jeanette, right in front of Mahalia, closed her eyes and listened. Josie shook his head as if he could scarcely believe his ears. After church they exclaimed, "We loved your singing, Halie. Won't you sing another song for us?"

Mahalia was always glad to sing for others, but she was especially pleased to have these cousins ask her to sing. "What song do you want me to sing?" she asked.

By this time most of the members of the congregation had walked on out the door, and Mahalia's father came over to talk with the group. "This daughter of yours surely has a beautiful voice," exclaimed Josie.

"Yes, Halie has a fine voice," said her father. "I'm mighty proud of her for the way she sings."

"We have just asked her to sing another song for us," explained Jeannette. "Will that be all right with you?"

"Of course," replied Mahalia's father. Then he turned to her and said, "Go ahead and sing another song for them, honey."

The organist, who was busy gathering up music

When Mahalia heard the familiar strains,
she started to sing.

at the organ, overheard this conversation. Without waiting to be asked, she sat down at the organ and started to play one of Mahalia's favorite songs. When Mahalia heard the familiar strains, she started to sing. At first, she sang softly, but gradually she lifted her head and sang with all the strength and feeling she could command.

Aunt Duke stood near the door of the church, waiting for the others to join her. She was impatient at having to wait, but her eyes filled with tears as she listened to Mahalia sing. She was as proud of Mahalia as if she were her daughter.

When the organist came to the end of the song, Josie motioned for her to keep on playing. At once she switched to another song which she knew that Mahalia liked. Mahalia picked up the new song and sang it with as much strength and feeling as the first song.

The singing went on and on until Mahalia's father said, "We must stop now and let the organist go home to her family."

Jeanette, Josie, and Mahalia's father went home with Aunt Duke for dinner. When they reached home, Aunt Duke asked Mahalia to help her prepare the food in the kitchen. The others sat and talked, mostly about Mahalia's singing. Mahalia wanted to stop and listen, but Aunt Duke kept telling her different things to do.

Soon after everybody was seated at the table, Josie said, "Jeannette and I would like to take Halie with us when we leave."

Mahalia's father looked up and shook his head in surprise. "I don't understand," he said. "Why do you want to take her with you?"

"Because of her beautiful voice," promptly replied Josie. "We believe that she belongs in show business.

We want her in our show. She could even help to sing the blues with Ma Rainey."

Uncle Emanuel spoke up. "Just what do you and Jeannette do in the show?"

"We have a comedy act," replied Josie. "We say and do things to make people laugh."

Jeannette went on to explain. "We travel from town to town and put on our show in a big tent. Usually we stay in each town several days and repeat the show several times."

Mahalia took a deep breath. She was too excited for words. She closed her eyes and tried to imagine what singing in a show would be like. She pictured herself standing in a bright spotlight, singing to a big crowd of people. Then later she could see herself bowing repeatedly as the crowd cheered wildly.

"Halie is still too young to travel or to be in show business," said her father.

"We would look after her just as if she were our own child," argued Jeanette. "You wouldn't have to worry about her."

She added, "Besides, she'll make good money and have some to send home to you."

Following this remark Aunt Duke's face took on a cold, hard look. Mahalia's father turned to her and asked, "What do you think of Mahalia going into show business?"

"I think 'No,'" replied Aunt Duke, almost before he had asked the question.

Jeannette looked over at Aunt Duke, surprised and dumfounded. "What did you say?" she asked. "Did I hear you correctly?"

"I said 'No,'" answered Aunt Duke flatly.

Mahalia looked at Aunt Duke. She could tell by the expression on her face that she was determined. Further arguing wouldn't change her mind, but Josie made one last attempt. "You're forgetting your own welfare," he said. "Halie will send you money from her singing."

Aunt Duke just sat straight and stiff in her chair. She shook her head back and forth and answered, "No."

Moments later, Jeannette and Josie bade the others good-by and left. Both Aunt Duke and Uncle Emanuel were glad to see them go.

Chapter 8

Joy and Sadness

Aunt Duke had a younger sister, Bessie, who was just seven years older than Mahalia. She went to school in the same building as Mahalia, and even though she was older, they became very close friends.

One spring when Mahalia was a young teenager, they got jobs doing housework together before and after school. They worked for a wealthy family, washing and wiping dishes and helping to look after several small children. Both were happy to be earning money.

On their first morning at work, they scraped off the breakfast dishes and washed and dried them together. The large number of dishes that the family had used surprised Mahalia. "How many people are there in the family?" she asked.

"I don't know," replied Bessie, "but they surely left a mess of dirty dishes for us to clean up."

"That's what I was thinking," said Mahalia.

Soon Bessie and Mahalia settled down to a routine

of working early mornings and late afternoons. One afternoon, when Mahalia returned home, she was surprised to find Cousin Fred sitting in the kitchen with Aunt Duke and Uncle Emanuel. "Hi, there, Halie," he called.

He jumped up from his chair and grabbed Mahalia and swung her round and round. She scarcely knew what was happening. Aunt Duke and Uncle Emanuel laughed, but offered no explanation.

Soon Mahalia learned that Cousin Fred had taken a job down at the docks and was planning to live with his parents. Early each morning he went to his work of loading and unloading riverboats. Each evening he put on his best clothes and went to nearby dance halls.

Cousin Fred was a handsome young man with neatly cut hair and pearly white teeth. He usually had a smile on his face and got along well with everybody.

One night Mahalia watched him curiously as he got ready to go out. He stood before a mirror, poured a sweet-smelling oil on his hands, and rubbed it into his hair. Then he combed his hair to make sure it was just so. "There, Halie," he exclaimed. "How does it look?"

He turned from the mirror and danced about the room while he put on a freshly starched shirt. He stopped dancing only long enough to fasten his big silk tie before the mirror. Finally he turned to Mahalia and said, "Honey-babe, I'm going to step out tonight! I'm going to paint the town."

Aunt Duke looked over sadly and asked him to hush up. She frowned as he started to leave, but he put his arm around her and said, "Good night, Ma. I'll see you later."

Both Aunt Duke and Mahalia worried whenever he left the house in the evening. They knew that he spent most of his time in dance halls, nightclubs, and gambling places, but constantly prayed that he would change his ways.

During that summer Cousin Fred bought a phonograph, and dozens of blues and jazz records. Mahalia loved the music and often played the records when Aunt Duke wasn't at home. Nearly every day she hurried up her housework so she could listen to them. She always felt guilty, however, because she knew Aunt Duke wouldn't approve.

Usually when she played a record, she sat on the floor in front of the phonograph. Sometimes she closed her eyes and absorbed the colorful, rhythmic sounds. At other times she sang along with the music or rocked herself back and forth to keep time.

One of her favorite records was "I Hate to See That Evening Sun Go Down." She soon learned both the words and the music. Then she sang the song whenever she played the record.

Early in the summer, Cousin Fred left as sud-

They marched back along the streets followed by people singing joyfully.

denly as he had come. Nobody knew exactly where he had gone, but word trickled back that he had gone to Kansas City. Mahalia found the house very quiet and lonely after he left. She was sure that Aunt Duke missed him, too, but she never let on.

That summer Mahalia got a job working with Aunt Bell, another sister of Aunt Duke. Aunt Bell was

a housemaid. Mahalia helped her do all kinds of work in the house.

Aunt Bell was a very efficient worker. She showed Mahalia how to prepare many tasty foods that Mahalia had never heard of before. She showed her how to make beds so that they looked neat and inviting, and how to iron clothes.

Mahalia liked working with Aunt Bell, but she

always was eager to return home. She loved to sit at the table and talk with Aunt Duke, Uncle Emanuel, and her brother Peter. This seemed to be the only time of day when they could relax and enjoy being together.

That fall, Mahalia entered the eighth grade and spent a busy year in school. The following spring, when she graduated, her school days were over. In New Orleans at that time, only certain kinds of jobs were open to African-American women. Going to high school would do her no good. She had to go out and get a full-time job somewhere in the city.

Soon she obtained work as a laundress. She put in ten hours a day and tried hard to do her work well. She was glad that she was earning her own living instead of depending on Aunt Duke.

As she washed and ironed, she wondered about her future. She wanted to become something more than a laundress. She realized that she didn't have enough schooling to become either a schoolteacher or a nurse.

At times her mind turned to show business, but she felt that it would be wild and wicked. She thought of the wailing and blaring sounds of the blues and jazz music coming from dance halls and nightclubs along the streets. The very thought of show business gave her a sense of wrongdoing that frightened her.

One night after she had gone to bed, she was awakened by unusual sounds coming from the kitchen. She got out of bed slowly and found Aunt Duke crying bitterly and pacing the floor. Her aunt's face was covered with tears.

She had never seen Aunt Duke like this before and wondered what had happened. When she reached the kitchen, she could hear Aunt Duke mumbling something under her breath, but she couldn't understand what she was saying. Finally she called out, "Aunt Duke, what's wrong? What's the trouble?"

Aunt Duke didn't answer. She merely handed Mahalia a crumpled sheet of yellow paper. Mahalia held the crumpled sheet in the moonlight coming through the window and could see that it was a telegram. Then she read the sad news that Cousin Fred was dead in Kansas City.

Aunt Duke arranged for Cousin Fred's body to be brought back to New Orleans for burial. The funeral services were held at the church, and a long wake was held prior to the services.

Cousin Fred had many friends in New Orleans. Several bands played soft music on the way from the church to the cemetery. At the cemetery people stood about in groups and listened with bowed heads.

After the burial services, as was the custom in New Orleans, the bands broke loose and played loud jazzy music. They marched back along the streets followed by people singing joyfully. The streets rocked with rollicking music, which Cousin Fred would have loved.

Chapter 9

Big Move to Chicago

Around the time Cousin Fred died, many African-Americans in New Orleans were moving north to live and work in Chicago. Several members of the church moved there and got well-paying jobs. They reported back to their relatives and friends.

Uncle Emanuel wanted to move to Chicago, but Aunt Duke wouldn't leave New Orleans. Finally he decided to go by himself to work for a while. Shortly after he arrived, he obtained a job as a bricklayer and started sending money back to Aunt Duke.

Uncle Emanuel came home again some months later. He told of many things that African-Americans could do in Chicago that they weren't allowed to do in New Orleans. They could ride in streetcars with white people, eat in restaurants with white people, and hold many of the same kinds of jobs as white people.

Two of Aunt Duke's younger sisters, Aunt Hannah and Aunt Alice, moved to Chicago and liked living there. One day Mahalia was surprised to receive a letter from them. In it, they invited her to come to live with them. They told her there were plenty of jobs. They also told her that she could attend a nursing school there.

Mahalia read the letter over several times. The possibility of going to a nursing school excited her. To her, this sounded almost like a dream come true.

She wasn't sure how Aunt Duke would feel about her going to Chicago. She took a deep breath and went to the kitchen to talk to Aunt Duke about it. "Aunt Duke," she said bravely, "Aunt Hannah and Aunt Alice have invited me to come live with them in Chicago. May I go?"

Aunt Duke didn't answer but kept on working as if she hadn't heard. She pointed to a bag of sweet potatoes and said, "Get six or eight of those sweet potatoes ready to cook." She paused for a moment and then added, "I don't understand why you would want to go to Chicago."

Mahalia obediently did as she was told. After she had finished peeling the potatoes, she decided to try again. "I want to go to Chicago so I can attend a nursing school," she explained. "Then maybe I can become a nurse in Chicago."

Aunt Duke looked at Mahalia coldly. "Well, you had better forget about all that nursing business and keep your job right here in New Orleans," she said firmly.

Mahalia felt hurt but said nothing. She had hoped that Aunt Duke would approve of her wanting to train to become a nurse. Even though her aunt objected, she made plans to go to Chicago when she could pay her own fare.

During the following months, she saved as much money as she could to help pay her railroad fare to Chicago. That winter, Aunt Hannah came to New Orleans for a visit. While she was there Mahalia decided to go to Chicago with her.

Though Aunt Duke was still against Mahalia going, she went to the railroad station to see her off. When Mahalia started to board the train, Aunt Duke threw her arms tightly around her. "Be careful up there in Chicago," she warned sadly. "Go to church and be a good girl."

"Oh, I will, Aunt Duke," called Mahalia. "Don't worry about me."

For two nights and one day, Aunt Hannah and Mahalia sat in a coach seat on their long train ride to Chicago. They were surrounded by bundles and had a basket of food which Aunt Duke had prepared for them to eat along the way.

At first Mahalia was excited to be riding on the train, but later the train ride became boring, and

Mahalia kept asking when they would reach Chicago. She was eager to get started with her new life there. Finally Aunt Hannah said, "Well, our trip is almost over. We can begin to gather up our things."

Aunt Hannah started to stack up the bundles to carry from the train. She pulled an old sweater from a shopping bag and handed it to Mahalia. "Here, put this sweater on under your coat," she ordered. "You'll find the outside air very cold here in Chicago."

When Mahalia stepped into the wintry air on the covered platform outside, she thought that Chicago must be the coldest place in the world. Aunt Hannah led the way along the crowded platform to the station. Mahalia followed as closely as possible, afraid that she might get lost. "We'll go directly to the taxicab stand in front of the station," said Aunt Hannah.

Outside a blizzard-like snowstorm was sweeping through the city. Aunt Hannah didn't seem to mind either the wind or the snow, but Mahalia could hardly get her breath or see where she was going. "Wait, Aunt Hannah!" she called frantically. "I can't keep up with you." Aunt Hannah stopped for a moment while Mahalia tried to get her breath.

When they reached the taxicab stand, there were no cabs there. "We'll have to wait until a taxicab drives in," said Aunt Hannah. "Put down your things and rest."

When Mahalia stepped into the wintry air on the covered platform outside, she thought that Chicago must be the coldest place in the world.

Mahalia gasped for breath and dropped all her bundles. She wiped her face with a handkerchief and, peering through the falling snow, caught her first hazy glimpse of Chicago. Across the street she could see a long row of tall buildings jutting into the sky. Somehow this made her forget the bitter cold. She felt excited and happy just knowing she was in Chicago.

Soon a taxicab came, and Aunt Hannah put their bundles inside. Then she stepped to one side and motioned for Mahalia to get in. Mahalia suddenly noticed that the driver of the taxicab was a white man. She grabbed her aunt's arm and said, "Look at the driver. We can't ride in this cab."

"Go on and get in," ordered Aunt Hannah. "Remember we're in Chicago."

The taxi driver took them over busy streets and boulevards to the apartment building where Aunt Hannah and Aunt Alice lived. Mahalia was awe-struck when she first saw this large brick building with an ornate iron fence in front. She had never imagined living in a fine building like this. Mahalia now lived on the South Side of Chicago. At the time, it was the second-largest African-American community in the United States. Only New York City's Harlem was larger.

A few days after Mahalia arrived in Chicago, Aunt Hannah fell ill, and Mahalia had to go to work. She got a job as a laundress on the North Side of Chicago. She felt disappointed, because it dimmed her hopes of getting training to become a nurse.

Mahalia found the weeks that followed long and tedious. She had to get up early and take a long ride to work on an elevated train. As she rode this train between tall, dark buildings, she felt as if she were trapped in a prison. Many times she wished she were back home.

Gradually she got to know and to like Chicago. She found many new friends to take the place of her old friends in New Orleans. Most of these new friends were in the nearby church, which she attended regularly with Aunt Hannah and Aunt Alice.

After the preacher and choir director heard Mahalia sing with the congregation, they invited her to sing in the choir. During her first practice session, the choir director had the members sing, "Hand Me Down a Silver Trumpet, Gabriel." Mahalia sang this song with her usual strength and fervor, and completely forgot she was singing with others.

Suddenly the choir director held up his baton to stop the singing. Mahalia felt sure that he was displeased with her for singing so loudly. She wished she could sink through the floor.

The choir director asked her to come forward. Now she was certain that he intended to punish her in some way or other. Instead he smiled and said, "You have a beautiful voice and I would like to hear you sing that song again all by yourself."

Mahalia was still nervous but felt greatly relieved. At first she held down her voice and sang softly, but gradually she gained confidence and sang with more and more vigor. Finally she threw back her head, closed her eyes, and sang at full volume.

The members of the choir were astonished by her singing. The choir director walked briskly over to her and said, "I congratulate you, Miss Jackson. From now on you will be a soloist in our choir."

The members of the choir now came forward and crowded around her. One after another, they congratulated her. One member said, "Your singing brings joy to us all."

When Mahalia left the church, she felt elated to be treated so warmly by the choir director and choir members. From this time on, she looked upon her neighborhood church as a haven of happiness in Chicago.

Chapter 10

Starting a Singing Career

Week after week and month after month, Mahalia continued to work as a laundress on the North Side of Chicago. She willingly worked hard to help her aunts with their living expenses, but still hoped sometime to attend a nursing school.

Each weekday she got up before sunrise to ride the elevated train to work. There, she stood continually by a tub, scrubbing dirty pieces of laundry, or by an ironing board, flattening out wrinkles or putting in creases. By evening she was so exhausted that she could scarcely drag her feet up the stairway to take the train home. She always had to stand, because it was too crowded for her to find an empty seat.

The train reached her stop and Mahalia jumped off. As soon as she reached the bottom of the steps from the elevated station, she rushed to the church. The church building was open almost every evening through the week, and Mahalia looked forward to stopping for awhile on her way home. There were many meetings, social gatherings, and the Wednesday evening prayer services. Most important to Mahalia, the church choir rehearsed several evenings.

During the choir rehearsals, Mahalia practiced singing both her solos and the songs she sang with others. Also, she had to practice singing in special duets, trios, and quartets. Sometimes, she sang either by herself or with others, just for the joy of singing.

Gradually, through her church activities, Mahalia built up a larger and larger circle of friends. She became so happy living in Chicago that she no longer thought of going back to New Orleans to live. Someday, however, she hoped to go back for a visit.

In the early 1930s, soon after Mahalia moved to Chicago, a great financial depression swept across the country. Banks failed, factories closed, and many workers lost their jobs. People lacked money to pay rent, buy food, and meet other expenses of living.

The Great Depression, as it was called, was especially hard on the African-American community in Chicago. They were among the first in the city to lose their jobs. Many had to find cheaper places to live, and others had to sell their cars and other belongings in order to buy food. Some lost their savings, because many of the banks went out of business.

At first, Mahalia was not affected. However, she

Late one afternoon as she returned from work, she found a long line of men and women waiting in front of a bank.

knew something terrible was happening, though she did not understand all the workings of the business world. Late one afternoon as she returned from work, she found a long line of men and women waiting in front of a bank. A big sign on the front door of the bank read, "Closed."

As Mahalia went by, she stopped to talk with some

of the people. One woman, whose face was drenched with tears, said, "The bank has closed and I can't get in to take out my savings."

"Well, you can get your money when the bank opens," said Mahalia.

"What!" exclaimed a man. "This bank will never open. Her savings are gone."

"How can they be gone?" asked Mahalia. "If she

put money in savings in the bank, the bank is still saving her money, isn't it?"

"Oh, no," explained the man. "The bank paid out all the money it had and then closed its door. The rest of us have lost our money."

Many of the women, and even some of the men, were in tears. Some were trying to console one another by talking. "We have lost both our savings and our jobs," they cried. "What can we do?"

Mahalia then went on to the church. When she stepped inside, she found another pitiful group of people. "I lost my job today," said a thin, neat-looking young man. "So did I," said another.

Before long the Depression hit Mahalia. She had to work longer hours and receive less money. Each afternoon when she returned home, she found people aimlessly walking the streets with no place to go. Some were begging to get a few pennies to buy a bite to eat.

After a few months, welfare agencies began to set up soup kitchens, where they passed out free soup to hungry people. One cold, snowy winter afternoon, Mahalia found a long line of people waiting outside a soup kitchen near her home. Most of them were shaking from standing for several hours in the cold wintry weather. Some prayed that the soup would last until they could go inside the building to get some.

Mahalia reached in her pocket and pulled out a wrinkled dollar bill and a few coins. She figured that she had enough money to purchase a few things at a grocery store. Then she called out to several nearby persons, "Come home with me and let me feed you."

Five or six adults and three or four half-grown children followed her. She purchased some meat, potatoes, and vegetables, and cooked a big supper. The people thanked her tearfully, wondering when they would have an opportunity to eat a good meal again.

Mahalia's close friends in Chicago included Prince, Robert, and Wilbur Johnson, who were sons of the preacher at the church. During the Depression, these three young men, Mahalia, and another young lady named Louise Barry formed a quintet which they called the Johnson Gospel Singers. They sang regularly at the church and attracted wide attention. Soon people began to come from all over the South Side to hear them sing.

Before long other churches on the South Side, and later churches all over Chicago, invited them to come and give concerts. In many cases they sang to help churches raise money.

During or after the concerts, the church officials took up collections. Then they took out part of the money for themselves and gave the rest to the members of the quintet. Sometimes the five singers earned as much as $1.50 apiece.

Later the Johnson Gospel Singers began to receive invitations to sing outside Chicago, in Illinois, Indiana, and Michigan. People liked their spirited, rhythmic singing because it helped them to forget their gloom over the Depression. Several times as Mahalia traveled about with the quintet, people asked her whether she had ever taken singing lessons. One day she and one of her friends decided to take lessons from a noted voice teacher on the South Side.

The teacher talked with them briefly and asked them to sing for him. First he took Mahalia to the piano and asked her to sing. She started to sing in her usual spirited manner, but almost immediately he stopped her and said, "That is not the way to sing this song. Let me show you how."

He then sang the song in a much slower rhythm and far more softly than Mahalia had sung it. "Now sing the song again and try to sing it just as I've shown you," he said.

Mahalia clasped her hands in front of her, ready to sing again. At first she sang slowly and softly just as the teacher had shown her, but soon she bounced back into her old way of singing. "No, no, no," shouted the professor. "You're ruining the song."

Next the teacher asked Mahalia's friend to sing

the song. She sang it slowly and softly, the same as he had sung it for Mahalia. When she finished, he said, "That was beautiful. You sang the song just right."

The teacher now turned to Mahalia and said, "You shout too much when you sing. For a white audience, you'll have to cut out your shouting and learn to sing more softly and slowly."

Mahalia was greatly disappointed with this criticism and felt that her way of singing the song was better than the professor's way. It was Mahalia's one and only singing lesson.

Chapter 11

Mahalia Sings as a Soloist

All the members of the Johnson Gospel Singers held regular jobs. They had to work to earn a living because they didn't make enough from their singing. Often when they had an engagement to sing, only some of them could go. The others had to go to work.

One evening when they had said they would sing at a church in Chicago, four of them had to work, and only Mahalia could go. When she arrived at the church all by herself, the pastor was worried. "Where are the other members of your group?" he asked.

"They couldn't come because they had to go to work," replied Mahalia. "I hope you won't object to my singing alone for your audience."

"Oh, no," replied the pastor nervously, "but I'll have to make an explanation to the people. We had announced that there would be five of you here to sing tonight."

Moments later the pastor led Mahalia up to the

Mahalia stood by the organ, clasped her hands in front of her, and sang with all the strength and feeling possible.

front of the church by the organ. "Ladies and gentlemen," he apologized to the audience, "I regret to announce that four members of the Johnson Gospel Singers had to work this evening and couldn't come to sing. The only member present is Mahalia Jackson, who will sing for us as a soloist this evening."

Mahalia stood by the organ, clasped her hands in front of her, and sang with all the strength and feeling possible. The members of the audience fell into the spirit of her singing and clapped their hands and stamped their feet to the rhythm. The pastor beamed with joy as he listened to the music and watched the happy expressions on the faces of the audience.

After the concert, the church people crowded around Mahalia to praise her. "Your singing lifted my spirits right up," exclaimed an old white-haired lady.

"Yes, I could hardly keep from coming up here and singing right along with you," said a well-dressed man.

The news of Mahalia's singing spread, and she began to receive invitations to sing as a soloist at other African-American churches on the South Side. The pastor of one church after another said to her, "Won't you come to my church to sing?"

Mahalia liked to sing to African-American congregations because she felt they understood her singing. She sang in most of the African-American churches in Chicago, and soon began to sing in other cities. Within a few years she was traveling throughout the entire country to sing. Night after night she sat on trains to travel from one city or town to another.

One trip to a town in Missouri was typical. She had agreed to sing at a church there for several evenings in a row. The pastor met her at the train station. "Welcome, Miss Jackson," he said. "My wife and I have arranged for you to stay in our home while you are here."

That evening, the pastor and his wife took Mahalia to the church to give her first program. The church was packed with people eagerly waiting to see her and to hear her. Each person had paid a nickel admission to attend the program.

Mahalia sang four nights in a row at the church, and each night more people came to hear her. On the last night they stood in the aisles and every available spot inside the church. Others stood outside and listened through the open windows and door.

Wherever she was, when Mahalia started to sing, the whole church rocked to the rhythm of her singing. People in the audience clapped their hands and stamped their feet to the beat of gospel music.

Even though Mahalia traveled widely, she barely earned enough money to pay her expenses. Between trips she always tried to work to earn money. She had to give up her job as a laundress because she was away too much of the time. Later she obtained a job as a maid in a hotel. Occasionally she cleaned as many as thirty-three rooms a day. She worked at this job every day for two years, when she wasn't traveling.

Besides singing in churches, she sometimes sang at church conventions. At one convention, she was scheduled to sing with Professor Thomas A. Dorsey, who was becoming famous as a composer of gospel songs. Two of his most popular gospel songs were "Precious Lord" and "Peace in the Valley," which had sold by the thousands.

Mahalia was proud to appear on the same program with Professor Dorsey and was eager to talk with him. "You surely have composed some mighty good gospel songs," she said. "How long have you been writing?"

"I started my musical career playing the piano for Ma Rainey in her tent shows," he replied. "In those days I was known as Georgia Tom."

Mahalia remembered her father's cousins, who once had come to New Orleans with Ma Rainey's show. "Did you happen to know Jeannette and Josie Burnette when you were in Ma Rainey's show?" she asked eagerly.

"Sure," he answered. "They did a comedy act. We were in the same show."

Mahalia smiled. "Well, they were cousins of mine," she said. "Once when they came to New Orleans with Ma Rainey, they wanted me to go with them to sing in the show."

"I'm glad you didn't go," said Dorsey. "You don't belong in that kind of show. You're a gospel singer."

Even though gospel singers were popular, some preachers didn't approve of them. They were opposed to singing songs that led people to clap their hands and stamp their feet to keep time. They felt that such songs weren't dignified and should not be sung in a church.

One evening when Mahalia was singing gospel songs in a church, the preacher stopped her. "This kind of singing is not fitting here," he exclaimed in an angry tone of voice. "You're just bringing jazz music into the church. I don't want the congregation to listen to such music."

These statements made Mahalia angry from head to foot. She stood erect and almost shouted back to the preacher, "Reverend, I have read the bible almost every day since I was a little girl." She started to sit down and then added, "You may not approve of gospel songs, but I believe they are what I should sing."

One summer Mahalia's grandfather, whom she called Grandfather Paul, came from Louisiana to visit. Mahalia and her aunts enjoyed his visit. While he was visiting, Mahalia wished she had a picture of him for her room. She persuaded him to get his picture taken at a local photographer's studio. She gave him money to pay for the picture, and he started out.

The weather was warm and he had to walk for blocks in the hot sun. Then after he reached the studio, he suffered a stroke.

When Mahalia and Aunt Hannah heard this shocking news, they rushed to the studio in a taxicab. They found Grandfather Paul, motionless and barely breathing, stretched out on the floor. Mahalia tried to talk with him, but he didn't even know she was there.

The photographer had already called an ambulance, which came and took him to the emergency room at the hospital. Aunt Hannah and Mahalia waited anxiously in the hall for someone to tell them about him. Finally a doctor reported, "He's seriously ill and may not live through the night."

Aunt Hannah was almost overcome with grief. "Oh, how I wish you hadn't wanted his picture!" she said. "Then this terrible thing might not have happened."

Mahalia felt so badly that she couldn't answer Aunt Hannah. She walked slowly down the hospital corridor until she came to an empty room. Sadly she went inside, fell on her knees, and prayed, "Please let Grandfather live."

She felt so guilty that she was eager to make some sort of sacrifice to save her grandfather. For years she had often gone to theaters to enjoy motion pictures and vaudeville shows. "If Grandfather lives," she prayed, "I'll never go to a theater again."

Grandfather stayed at the verge of death for several days. Then one day he started to get better. Several days later Mahalia joyfully helped him leave the hospital and return to the apartment. There he recovered rapidly and soon was able to return to Louisiana.

Mahalia never went to a movie or vaudeville theater again.

Chapter 12

Only Gospel Singing

One evening at a social event, Mahalia met an attractive, well-mannered young man named Isaac Hockenhull. He had attended Fisk University and Tuskegee Institute in the South, where he had majored in chemistry. Following graduation, he had come to Chicago to look for a job. Most of his friends called him "Ike."

When Ike first came to Chicago, he had hoped to get a job where he could use his training in chemistry. He looked far and wide, but good jobs were scarce because of the Depression He had finally obtained a job as a mail carrier, but occasionally when there was little mail to carry, he was laid off.

From time to time Mahalia happened to see Ike again, and soon he began to ask her out on dates. At first she hesitated to accept, because she felt so far beneath him in education. She couldn't understand why a man with a college education would want to associate with a young lady who never had gone beyond the eighth grade in school. Ike persisted, however, and she finally agreed to go out with him.

On their first date, she had very little to say. She was afraid that Ike wouldn't be interested in the simple things she would talk about. She actually was happy when the evening was over.

As they got to know each other better, Ike often told Mahalia about things he had read in books. Now and then Mahalia had to stop him and ask what a word meant. One time she said, "Ike, you know too much for me. I can't even understand you when you try to explain things to me."

Ike laughed. "Well, maybe I know a few things that you don't know, including big words, but I can't sing as well as you can. In fact, I can scarcely sing at all."

"You don't have to sing, because you can do many other things," said Mahalia, "but I have to sing. Singing is about all I can do. Besides, I love to sing."

"Yes, but you are foolish to keep on with that gospel singing," said Ike. "With your voice you could go into show business and make big money. You could become a great artist and sing in theaters all over the world."

"No!" exclaimed Mahalia. "I'm not interested in that kind of singing. I just want to sing the music I hear in church."

After nearly a year of courtship, Mahalia and Ike were married. At first they lived with Aunt Hannah, but they soon moved into a small nearby apartment. Mahalia was especially happy because this was the first time she had ever had a real home of her own. Now, at last, she would be free to come and go as she pleased.

After her marriage, she kept on with her gospel singing and made frequent trips out of town. Between these trips, she continued to work as a maid at a hotel. She felt fortunate to have this job, though she knew that sooner or later she would lose it because of her traveling. Every time she went on a trip, she had to ask other maids to take over her work.

After Ike and Mahalia were married, he tried to find a job to earn more money. He read want ads in newspapers and traveled about the city, trying to find a job where he could use his training in chemistry, but finally gave up. "I'll just have to keep on carrying mail," he said.

Always when Mahalia left on trips to sing, he was lonesome and wished she would give up singing and work steadily on her job at the hotel. Several times he pointed out that she would make more money by working steadily. If she still wanted to sing, he urged her to get a job singing in Chicago.

Ike was very proud of Mahalia's singing, but he had

Mahalia and Ike worked together for a time making and selling cosmetics based on ones his mother had made in St. Louis.

no feeling for gospel music. He couldn't understand why people clapped their hands or stamped their feet when she sang. He expected singers to stand on stages in theaters and sing to vast quiet audiences.

Mahalia and Ike worked together for a time making and selling cosmetics based on ones his mother had made in St. Louis. Ike took them door-to-door and Mahalia took them on her singing trips, but they soon realized that they could not make money selling the cosmetics.

About this time Louis Armstrong brought his band to Chicago to appear at a leading theater. He had heard of Mahalia, and while he was there, he found her and invited her to sing with his band. "I want you to sing the blues with us," he said. "You can start immediately and set your own salary."

"No," replied Mahalia. "I don't get the least bit of joy out of singing the blues, but when I sing gospel songs, I get thrilled through and through. That's my kind of singing."

Ike was greatly upset with Mahalia for refusing to accept this job with Louis Armstrong. He couldn't understand why she would turn down an opportunity to sing with one of the most famous bands in the country. He also couldn't understand why she would turn down the chance to earn big money for singing. To him she was wasting her time singing gospel songs for little or no money.

He had a heart-to-heart talk with her. "I'm afraid my life is doomed to failure," he said sadly. "When I graduated from college, I thought I could conquer the world. I came to Chicago with high hopes of getting a good job, but the Depression wiped out most of the good jobs. Then I tried to start that cosmetics business, but couldn't make it go. Right now, I guess I'm lucky to have my job as a mail carrier."

"Don't be discouraged," said Mahalia. "You're an intelligent, ambitious, well-meaning young man who deserves a better opportunity."

"But I'm fast losing my ambition," said Ike soberly. "I haven't anything to count on in the future, but you have your voice. I wish I could persuade you to quit that gospel singing and to start singing for money. You just turned down a wonderful offer to sing in Louis Armstrong's band. Well, if you don't want to go into show business, why don't you take a few singing lessons and become a concert artist? With your voice, you could become one of the greatest concert artists in the world."

At the mention of taking singing lessons, Mahalia threw up her hands. "Oh, no," she exclaimed to Ike. "Please don't ask me to take singing lessons. Once when a voice teacher tried to show me how to sing a song, I felt as if he were trying to strangle me. I just have to sing from my heart in my own way."

Ike gave up arguing. He went on carrying mail, and Mahalia went on traveling to do gospel singing. Once when Mahalia came back from a long singing trip, she found that he had lost his job as mail carrier. He had spent nearly all their money to pay the rent and to buy food. "Don't worry," said Mahalia. "I'll stay at home for a while and work steadily at the hotel until we catch up on funds."

But when Mahalia went back to the hotel, she found that she had lost her job, too. Slowly she walked back home to break the sad news to Ike.

Together they spread out and counted all their money. Mahalia sadly paced the floor, and Ike sat slouched forward in a chair with his face in his hands. "Oh, what shall we do?" asked Mahalia. "What shall we do?"

"You'll just have to start singing for money," replied Ike. "There's no other way."

Chapter 13

Singing My Own Way

Mahalia and Ike finished breakfast one day, and Ike began to look at the morning newspaper. Soon he cut out a clipping and handed it to Mahalia. "Look at this," he said. "Here is a real opportunity for you."

The clipping explained that auditions were being held to select a young lady to sing the leading part in a new jazz version of a famous comic opera called *The Mikado*. Mahalia read the clipping carefully and said, "Oh, no, I don't want a part in that show, or any other show. I just want to keep on singing gospel songs."

"You can get that part just by going over and singing," he persisted. "Then you will be started on a famous career. You'll travel all over the country and sing to thousands and thousands of people."

Mahalia sat quietly and held her head between her hands. She realized that somehow she and Ike had to find jobs to earn money, but she just couldn't bring herself to enter show business. Painfully she kept holding her head and saying, “No, no, no.”

Ike jumped up from his chair and shouted, “I don't see how you can just sit there and shake your head. Here's an opportunity for you to become a great artist. You have a special gift for singing. Now why don't you use it?”

“I am already using it,” cried Mahalia. “I'm using it to sing gospels.”

Following this statement by Mahalia, Ike grabbed his coat and hat and started to leave.

“Well, I'm going out to look for a job,” he said coldly, “and you had better do the same.”

Mahalia watched sadly as he left and felt guilty for not going out to look for a job, too. With great hesitation, she read the clipping again. It explained that tryouts for the show were being held at the Great Northern Theater.

Slowly she arose from the table and put on her coat. She patted down her hair but didn't even glance in the mirror to see how it looked. Mechanically she picked up the newspaper clipping and boarded a streetcar to go downtown.

When she reached the theater, she hardly could muster enough strength to go inside. She felt as if she were about to do something wrong. “May I help you?” asked a woman at the door.

“Oh,” replied Mahalia, still in a daze, “I came for

an audition for *The Mikado*."

"Where is your music?" asked the woman. "You'll need something familiar to sing."

Mahalia walked half-heartedly down the street to a music store. There, much to her surprise, she found a copy of the spiritual "Sometimes I Feel Like a Motherless Child." She purchased the copy and started slowly back to the theater.

This time the woman at the door took her to the audition room. The man in charge wrote down her name and the title of her song. He told her to take a seat in the back of the room and wait until he called her name.

One after another, the man called off names. Each time a young lady went down front and stood near the piano to sing her chosen song. Suddenly she heard the man call out her name, "Mahalia Jackson."

At once she felt cold and clammy. She walked slowly down front to the piano. Hesitatingly she handed the music to the pianist, who took it and started to play.

Mahalia clasped her hands, closed her eyes, and sang with feeling, as if she were the real motherless child in the song. Everybody in the audition room looked at her in wonder, entranced by her singing. The judges smiled and nodded their heads in approval.

As soon as Mahalia finished singing, she walked back to her seat and picked up her coat. She could tell that she had sung well, but she was eager to leave before the judges could tell her that she had got the part. She still didn't want the part.

For some time she walked the streets to try to get control of herself. At last she boarded a streetcar and rode back home. When she arrived, Ike was there waiting for her. He threw his arms around her and shouted, "They called to say you've been picked! I knew you would if you would only try!"

Ike whirled her round and round without giving her a chance to take off her coat. "They want you to start rehearsing your part tomorrow. At last you're on your way. Nothing can stop you now."

After this reception, Mahalia sank wearily into a chair. She didn't know what to say or do. Tears came to her eyes. Soon she asked, "How did you come out in looking for a job today? Did you have any luck?"

Ike stopped cold. "Yes, I got a job," he replied. "I'll make about as much as I did before. Of course, my job can't compare with yours."

"Please give me a chance to think," said Mahalia, starting to take off her coat. "Right now I'm all confused."

"But you don't have any time to think," said Ike. "You're supposed to start rehearsing tomorrow."

Mahalia went into the bedroom to hang up her coat. She realized that she faced making one of the

She lay down on the bed to read a few comforting passages from the bible.

most crucial decisions of her life, and that she must make it immediately. She lay down on the bed to read a few comforting passages from the bible and think about what to do.

Soon she felt that without question she must say, "No." She must not allow herself to be swayed by thoughts of singing either for fame or for money. She must sing only gospel music.

Bravely she climbed to her feet and went out to tell Ike. "I'm sorry, Ike, but I just can't accept that offer," she said.

From then on her marriage with Ike was never the same. Gradually they began to lead separate lives. Always, however, they remained close friends.

Eventually Mahalia began to worry about what to do if she had to give up gospel singing. She decided that she should be able to fall back on some other way of earning a living, if necessary. Finally in 1939, she attended a beauty school and started a beauty shop, which she called "Mahalia's Beauty Salon." A short time later, she opened a flower shop, which she called "Mahalia's House of Flowers."

Both the beauty salon and the flower shop became very popular on the South Side of Chicago. Women were proud to have their hair done at Mahalia's Beauty Salon. People purchased many flowers at Mahalia's House of Flowers for weddings and funerals. Often when a family purchased flowers for a funeral, Mahalia offered to sing at the services.

Mahalia also began to make records of some of her gospel songs. At first, her records were no more than a modest success, but she continued to record and perform.

During this period, World War II was in progress and many homes had young men away in the service. Mahalia's gospel singing was especially comforting to

Mahalia's gospel singing was especially comforting to these families. Somehow her singing gave them a new spirit of hope.

these families. Somehow her singing gave them a new spirit of hope.

One day a woman named Bess Berman, from Apollo Records, happened to hear Mahalia sing an old spiritual, “Movin’ on Up.” Miss Berman had never heard the spiritual before, but decided at once that it would make a good record. “How long have you been singing it?” she asked.

“All my life,” replied Mahalia. “Tonight I sang it just as I did down in New Orleans.”

“Well, you certainly sang it just right,” said Miss Burman. “I hope you’ll agree to make a record of it for me.”

In 1946, Mahalia recorded this spiritual. Within a few weeks it began to sell so fast that music stores couldn’t keep it in stock. The record sold over 2 million copies. Mahalia was on her way.

What Happened Next?

- Mahalia Jackson performed at Carnegie Hall in New York City in 1950.

- She toured Europe in 1952, but fell ill and had to return to the United States for a tumor to be removed.

- She appeared on Ed Sullivan's TV show in 1953, started a series of radio programs on CBS in 1954, and began to record with Columbia Records.

- She performed at events in support of the civil rights movement, including the famous March on Washington in 1963.

- She published her autobiography, *Movin' on Up*, in 1966.

- She died on January 27, 1972, in Chicago.

- In 1998, the US Postal Service issued a stamp in her honor.

The famous March on Washington in 1963.

Fun Facts About Mahalia Jackson

- Mahalia was the first gospel singer to have a regular show on network radio.

- In 1997, the Rock and Roll Hall of Fame chose her as an honoree.

- Mahalia sang for Presidents Eisenhower and Kennedy.

- Singer Billy Preston appeared with Mahalia in the movie St. Louis Blues in 1958 and went on to act as one of her accompanists. Later he played keyboard for the Beatles and became a rock-and-roll star in his own right.

- In describing Mahalia Jackson, Martin Luther King, Jr. said, "A voice like this comes, not once in a century, but once in a millennium."

Visit www.patriapress.com/jackson to learn more about Mahalia Jackson.

When Mahalia Jackson Lived

Date	Event
1911	Mahalia Jackson was born in New Orleans, Louisiana • Charles Lindbergh was the first to fly nonstop across the Atlantic Ocean in 31 1/2 hours. • Norwegian explorer Roald Amundsen became the first person to reach the South Pole.
1927	Mahalia moved to Chicago and began singing as a soloist in churches. • Ty Cobb became the first baseball player to have 4000 career hits. • The first talking movie, *The Jazz Singer*, was shown in theaters.
1935	Mahalia signed her first recording contract. • Rock-and-Roll king and legend Elvis Presley was born. • The Nazis enacted the Nuremberg Laws, which took away the civil rights of Jews in Germany.
1961	Mahalia Jackson performed at President John F. Kennedy's inauguration.

- A group of black and white men and women called Freedom Riders fought bus segregation in the South by riding buses from Washington DC to New Orleans. Their efforts forced the national government to take a stand against segregation.
- Alan Shepard became the first American in space.

1963 Mahalia Jackson sang just before Martin Luther King, Jr.'s famous "I Have a Dream" speech at the Lincoln Memorial in Washington DC.

- President John F. Kennedy was shot and killed in Dallas, Texas.
- The Beatles, one of the best known rock-and-roll bands of all time, became very popular in Britain. By 1964, they had a huge number of fans all over the world.

1972 Mahalia Jackson died of heart failure.

- Richard Nixon was re-elected President of the United States.
- The CD, or compact disk, was developed in the United States, eventually replacing the cassette.

Mahalia was the first gospel singer to have
a regular show on network radio.

What Does That Mean?

ardor (p. 48)—a lot of energy; intense excitement

burlap (p. 25)—a heavy, woven fabric used for bags

elated (p. 67)—excited, having high spirits

entranced (p. 93)—to be in a daze of delight or wonder

gaudy (p. 46)—showy, flashy, expensive looking

levee (p. 1)—a ridge of dirt along a river or the sea that helps prevent flooding

lye (p. 19)—a strong chemical-rich substance used in making soap

molasses (p. 8)—a thick syrup

okra (p. 18)—a green vegetable

ornate (p. 65)—decorated with much detail

phonograph (p. 55)—a record player

pulpit (p. 5)—a high platform from which a preacher gives a sermon

quintet (p. 73)—a musical group made up of five voices or instruments

sharecropper (p. 11)—a farmer who works on another man's land to grow crops for which he gets a place to live, food to eat, and a part of the crops' profits

stevedore (p. 2)—someone who loads and unloads ships

tedious (p. 66)—boring

About the Author

Montrew Dunham was born and reared in Indianapolis, Indiana. She received her B.A. degree from Butler University and her M.A. from Northwestern University. She has written numerous books for children, including *Oliver Wendell Holmes, Boy of Justice; George Westinghouse, Young Inventor; Anne Bradstreet, Young Puritan Poet; Abner Doubleday, Boy Baseball Pioneer; John Muir, Young Naturalist; Langston Hughes, Young Black Poet; Margaret Bourke White, Young Photographer; Roberto Clemente, Young Ballplayer; Neil Armstrong, Young Flyer; Thurgood Marshall, Young Justice;* and *Ronald Reagan, Young Leader.* She is also the author of *Downers Grove: 1832-1982* and author and narrator of several videos including *Images of the Past* and *The Life and Times of Dr. James Henry Breasted.*

Books in the Young Patriots Series

Volume 1 ***Amelia Earhart, Young Air Pioneer***
by Jane Moore Howe

Volume 2 ***William Henry Harrison, Young Tippecanoe*** by Howard Peckham

Volume 3 ***Lew Wallace, Boy Writer***
by Martha E. Schaaf

Volume 4 ***Juliette Low, Girl Scout Founder***
by Helen Boyd Higgins

Volume 5 ***James Whitcomb Riley, Young Poet***
by Minnie Belle Mitchell and Montrew Dunham

Volume 6 ***Eddie Rickenbacker, Boy Pilot and Racer***
by Kathryn Cleven Sisson

Volume 7 ***Mahalia Jackson, Gospel Singer and Civil Rights Champion*** by Montrew Dunham

Volume 8 ***George Rogers Clark, Boy of the Northwest Frontier*** by Katharine E. Wilkie

Volume 9 ***John Hancock, Independent Boy***
by Kathryn Cleven Sisson

Volume 10 ***Phillis Wheatley, Young Revolutionary Poet***
by Kathryn Kilby Borland and Helen Ross Speicher

Volume 11 ***Abner Doubleday, Boy Baseball Pioneer***
by Montrew Dunham

Volume 12 ***John Audubon, Young Naturalist***
by Miriam E. Mason

Volume 13 ***Frederick Douglass, Young Defender of Human Rights*** by Elisabeth P. Myers

Volume 14 ***Alexander Hamilton, Young Statesman***
by Helen Boyd Higgins

Watch for more **Young Patriots** Coming Soon
Visit www.patriapress.com for updates!

LaVergne, TN USA
17 October 2010
201136LV00002B/4/P